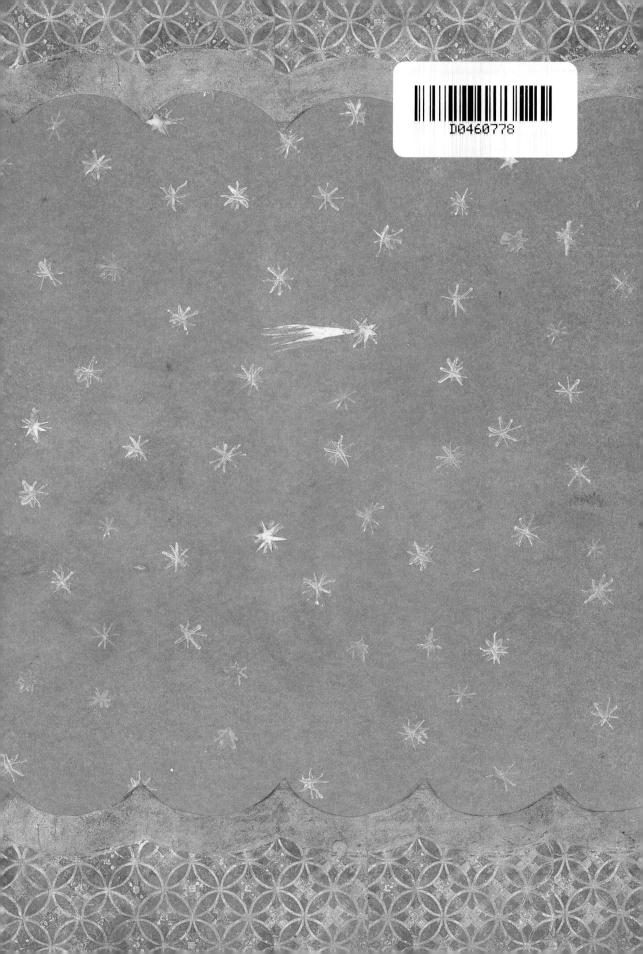

STORIES FROM THE LIFE OF JESUS

STORIES FROM THE LIFE OF JESUS

RETOLD FROM THE BIBLE BY

CELIA BARKER LOTTRIDGE

ILLUSTRATED BY

LINDA WOLFSGRUBER

WITHDRAWN

GROUNDWOOD BOOKS |HOUSE OF ANANSI PRESS
TORONTO BERKELEY

Groundwood Books / House of Anansi Press
110 Spadina Avenue, Suite 801, Toronto, Ontario M5V 2K4
Distributed in the USA by Publishers Group West
1700 Fourth Street, Berkeley, CA 94710

We acknowledge for their financial support of our publishing program the Canada Council
for the Arts, the Government of Canada through the Book Publishing Industry Development
Program (BPIDP), the Ontario Arts Council and the Government of Ontario through the
Ontario Media Development Corporation's Ontario Book Initiative.

ONTARIO ARTS COUNCIL
CONSEIL DES ARTS DE L'ONTARIO

Library and Archives Canada Cataloging in Publication
Lottridge, Celia B. (Celia Barker)
Stories from the life of Jesus / retold from the Bible by Celia Barker Lottridge;
illustrated by Linda Wolfsgruber.
ISBN-13 978-0-88899-497-4
ISBN-10 0-88899-497-4
1. Jesus Christ – Juvenile literature. 2. Bible stories, English – N.T.
I. Wolfsgruber, Linda II. Title.
BT302.L685 2004   j232.9   C2003-905014-9

Design by Michael Solomon
Printed and bound in China

To my mother, Louise Shedd Barker,
and to the memory of my grandfather, William Shedd
– CBL

To Claudia and Lorena
– LW

TABLE OF CONTENTS

FOREWORD

Jesus lived in a time of storytelling. Because few people could read, tradition, wisdom and news were all passed on orally.

Jesus himself did much of his teaching by telling stories. Crowds came to hear him because accounts of his teaching, healing and miracles spread through the countryside by word of mouth. As Luke tells us at the beginning of his gospel, after Jesus' death, eyewitnesses continued to tell of what they had seen during his lifetime. These stories were told and retold, and some were written down later for use in gatherings and services.

It is generally agreed by scholars that the gospels of Matthew, Mark, Luke and John were written a generation or two after Jesus lived. Each gospel was written in a different place for a particular group of people, but they all include stories that follow the course of Jesus' life as well as stories he told. The gospel writers were familiar with many stories told and written down about Jesus, and Matthew and Luke probably used the earliest gospel – Mark's – as one of their sources. Some stories appear in only one gospel while others are told by two or more of the authors, often with varying details. With each story I have noted every place a version of it occurs in the four gospels.

For this book I have chosen stories that have the satisfying structure of beginning, middle and end that characterizes oral stories. In some cases the chapter-and-verse organization later editors gave to the Bible has obscured this form, but as a storyteller myself, I can recognize a story that must have been shaped by being told many times.

All of the stories, including the ones Jesus told himself, took place in a particular part of the world at a particular time. They were rooted in people's real lives. Early listeners would have known about shepherds and sheep and what it was like to live in a small mud-brick house. Since we live in another time and another place, I have added some context to make the images in the stories clear.

Telling or reading a story aloud brings it to life. I hope that this book will inspire the telling and reading aloud of these wonderful stories, and that it will contribute to an understanding of the importance of story in the life of Jesus.

Celia Barker Lottridge

ELIZABETH AND MARY

In the days when Herod was the king of Judea, a priest Luke 1.5-66.

named Zechariah lived with Elizabeth, his wife, in the hill country near Jerusalem. They were good people and honored God in every way, but there was a sorrow in their lives. They were growing old and they had no children.

One day Zechariah went to the temple to burn incense, for that was his duty as a priest. He made his way through a throng of people praying in the courtyard and entered the silent temple. And there, standing on the right side of the altar of incense, was an angel.

Zechariah was overwhelmed with fear at the sight of the heavenly being.

But the angel said to him, "Do not be afraid, Zechariah. I have come to tell you that your prayers have been heard. Your wife, Elizabeth, will give birth to a son, and you will call him John. He will bring great joy to you and to many people, for he will be filled with the Holy Spirit and will turn many of the children of Israel toward their God."

"How can I believe what you say?" said Zechariah. "Look at me. I am an old man and Elizabeth is too old to bear a child."

The angel answered, "I am Gabriel. I have come from God

[*11*]

to give you this good news, but you refuse to believe me. Because of your lack of faith, Zechariah, your voice will disappear. You will not be able to speak a single word until everything I have told you has taken place."

And the angel was gone, before Zechariah could even try to speak.

The people in the courtyard began to wonder why Zechariah did not come out and give them his blessing. They waited, growing more and more puzzled until at last he came through the great door and stood gazing at them.

To their surprise he said nothing but only gestured toward them with his hands. When he opened his mouth as if to speak, no sound came out. The people were silent, too, for they knew from the wonder on his face that Zechariah had seen a vision.

He went home to Elizabeth and, writing on a tablet of clay, he told her about the angel and the son who would be born to them. Elizabeth could see that a wonderful thing had happened to Zechariah, and soon she was sure that what the angel had said was true. She knew that she bore a child in her womb, but for five months she did not tell anyone. She kept the knowledge in her heart and silently thanked God for giving her what she had desired for so long.

Now, as Elizabeth awaited the birth of her son, God sent the angel Gabriel to speak to a kinswoman of hers who lived in the town of Nazareth in Galilee. This woman was young, and she was soon to marry a carpenter named Joseph. She was called Mary.

Gabriel came to Mary one day as she sat alone. He said,

"Rejoice, for you are favored of God and you are blessed among women."

Mary could only gaze in awe at the angel. She did not know what his words meant.

But the angel said, "Mary, do not be afraid. God loves you and he is sending you a son. You will give birth to him and you will name him Jesus. He will be called the Son of God and will reign over a kingdom that will last forever."

Mary said, "How can this be? There is not yet a man to be father to my son."

The angel answered, "Your child will be God's son and he will be born of the Holy Spirit. Remember, Mary, with God nothing is impossible. Elizabeth, your relative in Judea, will also bear a child very soon, though she is an old woman."

Then Mary said, "Let it happen according to your word which comes from God." And the angel departed.

Mary immediately made plans to visit Elizabeth. She traveled to the village where Elizabeth and Zechariah lived and went to their house. Elizabeth welcomed her young kinswoman, and Mary returned her greeting with words of great affection.

As soon as Elizabeth heard Mary's voice, the baby in her womb moved. It felt to Elizabeth like a leap of joy, and she was filled with the spirit of God.

She said to Mary, "You are blessed and the child you will bear is also blessed. But why am I so fortunate that the mother of my Lord should come to visit me?"

Mary was amazed to be spoken to in such a way by a woman older and wiser than she. She stood silent for a

moment thinking of Elizabeth's words and of what the angel had said to her. Then she spoke.

"I praise the Lord for I am a humble woman born of common folk, yet he has given me such honor that my name will be remembered and praised by future generations. He has been merciful to those who recognize his power. He has scattered those who are proud in their hearts. He has put the mighty from their thrones. He has lifted the poor and hungry and given them what they need. He speaks to us as he spoke to our fathers, to Abraham and to all his descendants."

Mary stayed with Elizabeth for three months, and together they prepared for their babies to be born. Then she returned to her home in Nazareth.

The following month, Elizabeth gave birth to a son. Her relatives and neighbors rejoiced with her, and they came to the ceremony of circumcision on the eighth day after the child was born. All of them expected that he would be called Zechariah after his father, but Elizabeth said, "No, he must be called John."

They said to her, "It is the custom to call a child after one of his relatives. There is no one in your family called John. And what does Zechariah think? Zechariah, what name do you wish to give your son?"

Zechariah still could not speak, but he remembered what the angel had said. He took a writing tablet and wrote, "His name is John."

As soon as he had written these words his voice returned, because everything that Gabriel had foretold had now happened. Zechariah rejoiced, for at last he could speak aloud and praise God and welcome his new son, John.

The guests were awestruck by what they had seen, and they told their neighbors and friends. Soon all of the people of the hill country talked of what had happened to Zechariah and Elizabeth and wondered what kind of man John would become.

JESUS IS BORN

Matthew 1.20-21;
Luke 2.1-20.

CAESAR AUGUSTUS, Emperor of Rome and ruler of many lands around the Mediterranean Sea, wanted to know how many people lived within his empire. So he sent out a decree saying that every man must go to the place of his birth to be recorded in the census and that each one must bring with him all of his family so that they might be listed, too.

So it was that all over the great empire people traveled by foot, by donkey, by camel and by chariot to the towns of their birth to be counted.

One man who prepared for this journey was Joseph, a carpenter who lived in the little town of Nazareth in Galilee. He had been born in Bethlehem, called the city of David because the great King David had been born there long ago. Indeed Joseph was a descendant of David. And so Joseph traveled to Bethlehem to be enrolled in Caesar's census.

He did not go alone. Mary, his wife, made the journey with him, riding on their little donkey. Mary could not walk to Bethlehem, for she was expecting her first baby to be born very soon.

As they traveled, Mary and Joseph thought about this child. They knew that he would be a very special child because of the angel who had come to Mary. He had said, "The child who will be born to you is the Son of God. You must call him Jesus." The angel had given the same message to Joseph.

Neither Mary nor Joseph could imagine what it would mean to have such a child in their family. But surely, for his birth, Jesus would need shelter and warmth and peace.

When they arrived in Bethlehem it seemed that a place of warmth and peace was not to be found. The city was crowded with people who had come to be enrolled in the census. Even the inn had no room for them. Mary knew that her baby would be born very soon and she prayed while Joseph searched for a house that would take them in.

All he could find was a stable where cows and sheep were kept. But Mary did not mind. The stable was sheltered and quiet. Her baby would be born in peace.

Joseph lit a lantern and gathered clean hay to make a soft bed for Mary. On it he spread his cloak and the blanket he had brought. The cows and sheep stood close around and breathed their warm breath into the air.

And Jesus was born.

When Mary and Joseph looked upon his face for the first time, they thought he was the most beautiful baby they had ever seen, but he was also like every baby they had seen, waving his arms and legs and blinking his eyes in the lantern light. Mary held him for a long time. Then she took the soft cloths she had brought and wrapped Jesus carefully so that he was warm and snug. Joseph put clean hay in the manger that usually held the hay the animals ate, and that was Jesus' bed.

No one in Bethlehem knew of the wonderful thing that had happened. Even the animals were quiet so that Jesus and Mary could sleep while Joseph kept watch.

But God and the angels knew that the Son of God was born.

Not far from the town there were shepherds in the fields with their flocks. On this night, as on other nights, they were taking turns sleeping and watching over the sheep.

Suddenly the dark sky was filled with light so that all the shepherds awoke. As they gazed in astonishment, an angel appeared and spoke to them.

"Be not afraid," said the angel, "for I bring you joyful news. Tonight in the city of David a baby has been born and he is Christ, the Son of God. Go and find him. You will know him because he lies in a stable, in a manger, wrapped in swaddling clothes."

The shepherds were amazed. A child just born who was the Son of God? And that child lying in a stable, in a manger?

Then the sky was filled with angels singing, "Glory to God on high and peace on earth to people of good will."

The shepherds knew that they must find the newborn child. So they left their flocks and hurried to Bethlehem.

The town was quiet and the streets were empty. There was no one to answer the shepherds' question, "Where is the child we seek?"

They walked through the streets looking at each stable and cow shed, but all were dark and silent.

At last they saw a glimmer of light within a little stable.

They gently pushed open the door and saw Jesus lying in the manger with Mary and Joseph nearby.

Then the shepherds fell down and worshiped, for they knew that what the angel had told them was true.

When at last they went out into the town to return to their sheep, morning was brightening the sky and there were people in the streets. The shepherds told everyone they met of the wonders that had happened in the night, and all were amazed.

As dawn filled the stable with light, Mary looked at her son and remembered the joyous faces of the shepherds and the voices of angels in the quiet night, and she kept these memories in her heart.

THE MAGI COME TO
BETHLEHEM

I N A L A N D F A R F R O M J U D E A there lived men of great Matthew 2.1-23. wisdom who spent their lives studying the heavens. They believed that the patterns of the stars would tell them of happenings in distant places and in times to come. These men were called magi.

From their desert and mountain homes the magi saw a wonderful star – one they had never seen before. Night after night it shone, and each of the magi gazed at it and wondered what it might mean. They looked in ancient books and learned that such a star shining in the east meant that a new king had been born to the Jewish people.

And each of the magi decided that he must go to see this wonder for himself. And so they began their journeys. As they traveled they met up with one another and continued on together.

They spoke with everyone they met.

"Tell us," they said. "Where is the child who is born to be king? We have seen his star in the east and we wish to find him, to welcome him into the world with honor and gifts."

But no one could tell them where the new king lay.

At last they came to Jerusalem and asked at the inns and in the streets. The people of the city wondered at these questions and talked among themselves. At last the gossip about a new king reached King Herod, ruler of Judea, and he called together the chief priests and advisors of his court.

"Do you know of any prophecy that a new king will be born to the Jewish people?" he demanded. "Do you know where he will be born?"

They answered, "Yes, O king. It has been prophesied that out of the town of Bethlehem shall come a ruler who shall be like a shepherd to the people of Israel."

Now Herod was not pleased to hear that a new king might have been born, for he, Herod, was king and he wanted no other. He invited the magi to meet with him privately. He asked them about the star and the date of its appearance. Then he said, "Those who study ancient books tell me that this king will be found in Bethlehem. Go there and find him. Then return and tell me who he is so I, too, might go and worship him."

So the magi traveled toward Bethlehem. As they journeyed, the star moved before them, and they followed it until it stopped over a simple stable on a narrow street.

But the light of the star made everything beautiful, and the magi were filled with joy as they entered the stable and saw the little child with Mary, his mother. They fell on their knees and worshiped him. Then they opened the treasure boxes they had brought and gave him gifts made of gold and vessels filled with sweet-smelling frankincense and myrrh.

They rested then from their long journey, and as they slept a dream came to each one of them. When they woke they found that they had all had the same dream. It told them not to return to Herod.

"We must not speak with him," they said to each other. "Perhaps he wishes to harm this beautiful child. We will not travel through Jerusalem." And so they returned to their own country by another route.

Soon after the magi left, Joseph had a dream, too. He dreamed of an angel who said to him, "You and Mary must take your son and go to Egypt. You must stay there until I come again to tell you to return. Herod intends to find Jesus and kill him, for he wants no other kings in Judea."

Joseph woke Mary and told her of the dream. They quickly bundled Jesus up, packed their few belongings and took the road to Egypt, traveling as swiftly as they could.

When the magi did not return to Herod, he was furious. He remembered what they had said about the time when the star appeared, and he decided that this new king must be a boy no more than two years old. So he issued orders that all boy children in Bethlehem two years old and younger must be killed.

News of the decree traveled fast. Many children were hidden or sent away by their families, and the soldiers could not find Jesus, for he was safe in Egypt.

And there Mary and Joseph and Jesus stayed until the angel came again to Joseph in a dream and said, "Herod is dead. It is time for you to return to Israel. Go home to the town of Nazareth, in Galilee, for there you will be safe."

And so the boy Jesus lived and grew to manhood in Nazareth.

PASSOVER IN JERUSALEM

JESUS GREW UP IN GALILEE in the little hill town of Luke 2.40-51. Nazareth. He helped his father, Joseph, in his carpenter shop and played with the village children in the narrow streets. The teachers at the synagogue taught him to read, and he grew to be a thoughtful boy and strong.

When he was twelve years old his mother said to him, "Now you are old enough to go with your father and me to Jerusalem and take part in the Passover celebration."

Jesus helped Mary and Joseph load everything they would need onto their little donkey. Many of their neighbors joined them as they set out on foot for the holy city. It took a week to make the journey, and when they arrived they found the streets crowded with people from towns near and far.

There were ceremonies in the temple and feasting to celebrate the time long ago when the Israelites had been delivered from captivity in Egypt. People visited with friends and relatives from distant towns and explored the markets and other wonders of the city.

But Jesus did not join the lively crowds that thronged the streets of Jerusalem. His family didn't wonder where he was. They understood that he was a grown boy, and they supposed that he was enjoying a holiday.

But they were wrong. Jesus was spending his days at the temple listening to the learned teachers.

A week passed and it was time to return home. All the people from Nazareth loaded their donkeys and made ready for the journey. Joseph and Mary thought their son must be somewhere in the crowd, helping another family. They would meet up with him at the first camping place.

But when they arrived, Jesus was nowhere to be found. They asked all their relatives and friends but no one knew where he was.

They grew more and more worried. When was the last time they had seen their boy? It had been days.

Joseph and Mary could not sleep that night, and very early in the morning they set off for Jerusalem to search for their son in the winding streets and marketplaces. It was not until three days later that they found him in the temple, listening to the wise teachers and asking them questions. The teachers had questions for Jesus, too, and he answered with an understanding that astonished all the listeners.

Joseph watched for a minute. Then he went to Jesus and said quietly, "Come at once, your mother is waiting."

When Mary saw him she hugged him and said, "My son, we didn't know where to find you. Why didn't you tell us where you would be? We have been so worried."

Jesus smiled at her and said, "You should have known that I would be here. This is my Father's house."

Joseph and Mary were not sure what Jesus meant, but they were glad to take him home to Nazareth where he was again an

obedient son. But Mary remembered what he had said. And as he grew older, she sometimes thought of how the most learned scholars had listened to him when he was only twelve years old.

JOHN THE BAPTIST AND JESUS

As Jesus grew to manhood in Nazareth, John, the son of Zechariah and Elizabeth, was called by God to go into the wilderness of Judea to tell the people that they should prepare for a new leader and teacher who would come from God.

Matthew 3.1-17;
Mark 1.4-12;
Luke 3.1-22.

Like the ancient prophets, John dressed in rough clothes made of camel's hair, and he wore a leather belt around his waist. He lived on locusts and honey and wandered in wild places.

Many people came from Jerusalem and all of Judea to hear him preach. He told them all that they must give up their sinful ways and make a new commitment to God. He said that to show they truly repented and would leave all wickedness behind, they should come into the Jordan River with him. When they rose from the water the sins of their old lives would be washed away. This was called baptism, and so John came to be called John the Baptist.

The power of John's words drew people to him – even tax collectors and soldiers who were known to use their power to take money and goods from people. John told them all to give away what they did not need and to take nothing that

belonged to another. Even if they had lived wicked lives, God would forgive them if they repented and were baptized.

Some people began to ask him if he was the Son of God, the new leader that many were expecting.

John said, "One is coming who is more powerful than I. One so filled with the Holy Spirit that I am not worthy to untie the thong of his sandal."

Jesus heard that John was baptizing people in the Jordan River near the main road to Jerusalem, and he came to be baptized with the others. When John saw him coming, his great voice was silenced. He stepped away from the bank of the river, saying quietly, "Why do you come to me? I should come to you for baptism."

But Jesus said, "It is right for you to baptize me."

So John took him into the river and baptized him as he had so many other people. As Jesus came up from the water, the heavens opened and he saw the Spirit of God descending like a dove and coming to him. And a voice from heaven said, "You are my Son, my beloved Son, and I am well pleased with you."

IN THE WILDERNESS

Matthew 4.1-11;
Luke 4.1-30.

AFTER JESUS WAS BAPTIZED in the Jordan River, he felt the Spirit of God leading him into the wilderness of Judea where the sun was hot and there was little water. For forty days and forty nights he wandered in this wild land. He ate nothing, and his thoughts were all on God and what God wanted him to do.

The devil, the enemy of God, saw that Jesus was famished and decided that he might easily be tempted to go against the will of God. So he came to Jesus and put a row of stones before him.

"If you are the Son of God," he said, "command these stones to become loaves of bread. Why should you be hungry?"

Jesus looked at the stones and answered, "God has told us that bread alone will not keep us alive. We also need God's word to guide us and give us strength. I have God's word. It gives me what I need."

Then the tempter lifted Jesus into the air and carried him to Jerusalem, the holy city, and put him on the highest pinnacle of the temple roof and said to him, "If you are the Son of God, throw yourself down, for it is written that God's angels

will catch you and lift you up so that not even your foot will be dashed against the stone."

Again Jesus answered him, "We are told that we must not test God's powers. This is written and I will not do it."

So the devil took Jesus to the top of a very high mountain and, in an instant, showed him all the kingdoms of the world and their splendor.

He said, "All these I will give you, if you will fall down and worship me."

"Away with you, Satan," said Jesus. "Away with you! For we are told to worship the Lord our God and serve only him. I will not serve you."

Then the devil knew that Jesus would not be tempted to go against God's words, so he left him there in the wilderness. But angels came and brought him all that he needed.

Jesus left the wilderness knowing that God wanted him to go among the people to teach and tell them to come to God in a new spirit. So he returned to Galilee and went from town to town, speaking in the synagogues and reading from the scrolls of the prophets. Many came to hear him because he spoke with power and there was wisdom in his sayings.

When he arrived in Nazareth, the town where he had grown up, people had heard of his travels and his teaching and they came to listen to him. They were amazed at how well he spoke and they said, "Aren't you the son of Joseph the carpenter? How do you come to speak with such authority?"

Jesus said, "I know it is hard for you to believe that I will say anything important. Who pays attention to someone who grew up right next door? But, truly, you should listen to me." And he told them in the words of the prophets that if they would not listen to the word of God, then God would turn away from them.

The people of Nazareth did not like to hear this. They were so enraged that they pushed Jesus before them to the edge of town and tried to hurl him off a cliff. But Jesus did not fall. He simply turned away from the cliff. The crowd parted before him, and he made his way to the road and went on to the next town.

GATHERING THE DISCIPLES

Matthew 4.13-22;
Mark 1.16-20;
Luke 5.1-11, 8.1-3.

JESUS WENT TO LIVE IN CAPERNAUM, a little fishing village on the shore of the large lake that is called the Sea of Galilee. He wanted to tell people that it was time to give up their greedy and selfish ways, to care for one another and be faithful to God. "The kingdom of God is at hand," he said. He wanted everyone to be prepared.

When he was a boy in Nazareth Jesus had seen how busy men and women were with their work and their families. He knew that if he wanted all the people to hear his message, he must go to them in the places where they lived their day-to-day lives. So he walked from town to town in Galilee, teaching in the synagogues and also talking to people where they gathered and worked. News of this man, whose voice was strong and whose words painted pictures that everyone could understand, spread throughout the countryside. People began to wait for him and seek him out as he traveled.

Among the crowds of men and women, Jesus searched for a few whose spirit would allow them to leave their old lives and follow him. These people would help him in his work, learn from him and finally become teachers themselves. They would be his disciples.

One morning a great crowd came to hear Jesus speak on

[38]

the shore of the Sea of Galilee near Capernaum. They pressed close around him, and he looked for a place to sit so that everyone could see and hear. There were two fishing boats drawn up on the shore while the fishermen washed their nets. Jesus asked one of them, a man called Simon, to take him a little way out from shore in one of the boats. Then he sat in the boat and spoke to the people.

When he had finished, he said to Simon, "Put the boat out into deep water and let down your nets. Catch some fish!"

The fisherman answered, "We have been fishing all night and not a single fish has come into our nets. But we will try again if you say we should."

So Simon and his brother Andrew took the boat out into the lake, and Jesus went with them. Almost as soon as the nets were in the water they were so filled with fish that they were beginning to break. The men signaled to their partners, James and John, the sons of Zebedee, to bring out the other boat. Soon both boats were so heaped with fish that they were in danger of sinking.

All four fishermen were amazed at the size of the catch, but Simon, who was also called Peter, fell down at Jesus' knees and said, "You should go away from me, for I am a sinful man."

Jesus said to him, "Do not be afraid. Leave your nets and come with me. I will teach you to bring people to the truth instead of fish into nets." And when they had brought their boats to shore the four men left everything and followed him.

One by one and two by two Jesus gathered more disciples, until there was a group of twelve. They were the ones who were

always with him, who helped him as best they could. They tried to understand his teachings and have faith in him.

Others, too, went with Jesus as he traveled and taught. Mary of Magdala, Johanna and Susanna and many others helped him in his work. Sometimes his mother and some of his brothers were there, too. Jesus said that all of them, the disciples and those who gave their time and their possessions to help him, were his family.

THE WEDDING AT CANA

John 2.1-11

JESUS AND HIS MOTHER MARY and the disciples were all invited to a wedding in the village of Cana. After the marriage ceremony the feasting and visiting lasted several days. There was a steward in charge of the celebration to make sure that the guests had plenty of food to eat and that their cups were filled with wine.

But the steward had many things to attend to, and it was the servants who realized that the wine was gone long before the guests were ready to go home. Mary noticed their worried looks and she overheard them saying, "What shall we do? There is no more wine."

She went to Jesus and told him what had happened. "They say that there is no more wine. It's too bad. The guests will say the bridegroom has not been a good host, and he will feel ashamed."

Jesus answered, "Why are you telling me about this? It is not yet time for me to perform miracles." But he smiled and looked around the room.

He saw six large stoneware jars used to hold water so that people could take part in the ritual of purifying their hands and dishes before eating. Now the jars were empty. Jesus said to the servants, "Fill the jars with water right up to the brim."

The servants did as he asked. It took a while. Each jar was nearly waist high and held several buckets of water.

When every jar was full, Jesus said, "Now take a cup of water out of one of the jars and serve it to the steward."

The servant who filled the cup opened his eyes wide, for he saw that the water was no longer clear but deep red. He took the cup to the steward who was not surprised, since he did not know that the wine had run out. But when he drank from the cup he, too, opened his eyes wide. He called to the bridegroom and said, "This is very good wine. Most often people serve the good wine first and save the poor wine for later when it won't be noticed. But you have kept the best wine until now."

The bridegroom did not know what to say. He had provided only one ordinary wine for the feast. And now six jars were filled with the best wine he had ever tasted.

The servants looked at each other and at Jesus. No one else except Mary knew where that wine had come from. Later, when she told the disciples what her son had done, they began to know that God had given great powers to this man they had been called to follow.

THE SERMON ON THE MOUNT

Matthew 5.1-7.28

PEOPLE CAME FROM FAR AWAY to hear Jesus teach in Galilee. They came from Jerusalem, from all of Judea and even from beyond the Jordan River.

One day, seeing that a great crowd was waiting to hear him, Jesus went up on the slope of a mountain. He sat down with his disciples gathered around him and began to speak.

"You may feel that you are humble and poor, you may be discouraged and sad, you may think that your hopes for justice and peace will not be fulfilled. I have good news for you! Listen.

"Blessed are those who are poor in spirit, for theirs is the kingdom of heaven.

"Blessed are those who feel sadness, for they will be comforted.

"Blessed are the gentle, for they will inherit the earth.

"Blessed are those who hunger and thirst after what is right, for they will be satisfied.

"Blessed are the merciful, for they will be treated with mercy.

"Blessed are those who are honest and true, for they will see God.

"Blessed are the peacemakers, for they will be called the children of God.

"Blessed are those who are persecuted for doing right, for theirs is the kingdom of heaven.

"I am here to tell you that you are the light of the world. Remember, no one lights a lamp and then hides it under a basket. The lamp is put on the table so that its light can shine out into the whole house. In the same way, let the spirit of your love and the good that you do shine out to give joy to the people around you and glory to God in heaven."

Jesus told his listeners that he had not come to overthrow the laws that had stood for centuries, but to teach people to understand the spirit of the laws, not just the words.

"You have heard it said, 'You shall not murder,' but I say beyond that, if you are angry with someone or if you insult someone, you must make peace or you will be punished.

"You have heard the old saying, 'An eye for an eye and a tooth for a tooth,' but I say to you, do not take revenge. If someone strikes you on the cheek, turn your other cheek to him. If someone forces you to go one mile, go a second mile.

"You have heard, 'Love your neighbor and hate your enemy.' I say to you, God sends the sun to shine on good and bad people alike, and you must love your enemies as well as your neighbors. If you are friendly only to your brothers and sisters, what credit is that to you?

"Do good things quietly so that only God will know. Do not make a great show of giving money to the poor or praying or fasting.

"Do not gather together many possessions that will only wear out or be stolen. Your heart will be where your treasure is, so gather treasures of the spirit that moths and rust and thieves cannot touch. You cannot serve God and wealth at the same time.

"Do not worry about having enough food to eat or clothes to wear. Look at the birds of the air. They do not grow food for themselves. God provides it. And think of the lilies of the field. They do not spin and weave and make clothes for themselves, and yet they are more beautiful than even the great King Solomon in all his glory. If you live and work toward the kingdom of God, everything you need will be given to you.

"There is no use worrying about what will happen tomorrow. Think of what is happening today. Ask God for what you need and it will be given to you. Search for what is important and you will find it. If a door seems closed to you, knock and it will be opened. If a child asked you for bread, would you give the child a stone? If you, who are not perfect, know how to give the right gift to a child, how much more will God, who is perfect, give good things to those who ask him!

"Remember, always treat other people as you want them to treat you. This is the law and this is what we are taught.

"I know that many of you who show me great reverence will not do the hard things that God asks of you. The way of goodness is not the easy way. But if you hear my words and act upon them, you will be like a wise man who built his house on solid rock. The rain fell and the floods came and the wind beat upon the house but it did not fall because it was built upon a rock. If you hear my words but pay no attention to them, you will be like a foolish man who built his house on sand. The rain fell and the wind blew and the house fell with a mighty crash."

When Jesus had finished, the listeners were filled with awe, for he had spoken to them with conviction – not like a person merely reciting what had been written, but like one who had considered and believed what he said.

THE SAMARITAN WOMAN

John 4.3-30, 4.39-42.

ON A JOURNEY from Judea to Galilee, Jesus and his disciples passed through Samaria. As they neared the city of Sychar they knew they were crossing land where their ancestor Jacob had once pitched his tent and built an altar. When he died, Jacob gave that plot of ground to his beloved son, Joseph, but in time the whole region had become the country of Samaria. Jews seldom came that way, for they felt that the Samaritans no longer worshiped as they should.

Near noon the travelers came to a well not far from Sychar. Jesus, who was tired from teaching the crowds who came to hear him, decided to rest there while the disciples went into the city to buy food.

Before long a Samaritan woman came to draw water from the well. As she prepared to lower the bucket, Jesus said to her, "Would you give me a drink?"

The woman was surprised.

"How is it that you, a Jew, ask me, a woman of Samaria, for water? As you must know our peoples do not share food or drink."

Jesus said, "I am a thirsty traveler asking you for water from the well. But if you knew who I am, you would ask me for a drink and I could give you living water."

The woman said, "But, sir, where is this living water you can give me? There is no running water in this land. Are you greater than Jacob who drew water from this well for his children and his flocks to drink? This is a deep well and you do not even have a bucket. How can you give me water?"

Jesus answered, "This is a good well. But anyone who drinks its water will be thirsty again. Those who drink of the living water that I give them will never be thirsty again. That water will be the gift of God, like a gushing spring giving them eternal life."

"Give me some of this living water you speak of so that I will not have to come here time after time to draw water."

Jesus said, "I will tell you more. Go and call your husband and come back."

"I have no husband," said the woman.

"I know that you have no husband," said Jesus. "You have been married five times but your husbands have died and you have not been able to marry another man."

The woman stared at him. "You know everything about me," she said. "You must be a prophet. Tell me then, my people say that our ancestors worshiped on this mountain and we worship here today. It is our holiest place. Your people say that Jerusalem is holiest of places. Who is right?"

Jesus said, "The time is coming when you will worship neither on this mountain nor in Jerusalem but in spirit and in truth. The place is not important. The spirit is what matters. I have come to give this message to you."

Just then the disciples came back from the town. They saw Jesus talking with the woman and they were astonished. Not only was this woman a Samaritan, it was not the custom for a man to speak with any woman he did not know. But they waited and said nothing.

The woman left her water jar by the well and hurried back to the city. As she went she told the people she met, "I have spoken with a man at the well who knows everything I have done. He told me wonderful things. Do you think he could be the Messiah, the one God has sent to save us? Come and see him!"

When they heard what the woman said, people wanted to see this man for themselves. So they came to Jesus and asked him to teach them. He stayed with them for two days and many believed his message.

As Jesus left Sychar to go on to Galilee, these Samaritans said to the woman who had first met him by the well, "We came to hear Jesus because of what you told us. Now we have heard for ourselves and we believe because of his words."

TAKE UP YOUR BED AND WALK

Mark 2.1-12;
Luke 5.17-26.

MANY PEOPLE CAME to Jesus' house in Capernaum to hear his teaching. The house, like others in the town, had only one room. It was built of sun-baked brick, and the roof was flat and made of sticks covered with packed earth. There was a square hole in the center so that smoke from the cooking fire could escape and light could come into the house. The people could climb a staircase up the outside wall of the house to sleep on the roof on hot nights, or they could spread fruit there to dry in the sun.

Often Jesus' house became so crowded that people would stand outside waiting to get in. On such a day four men came through the narrow street carrying their friend on a sleeping mat because he was ill and could not move. They were hoping to ask Jesus to heal this man. When they saw the people packed around the door, they knew that they had to find another way into the house.

They managed to reach the outside staircase and carry their friend up to the roof. There was no smoke coming through the hole so they looked down and saw Jesus speaking with one person after another. Carefully they removed sticks and dirt to make the hole larger. Then they grasped the corners of the sleeping mat and together they lowered their friend down into

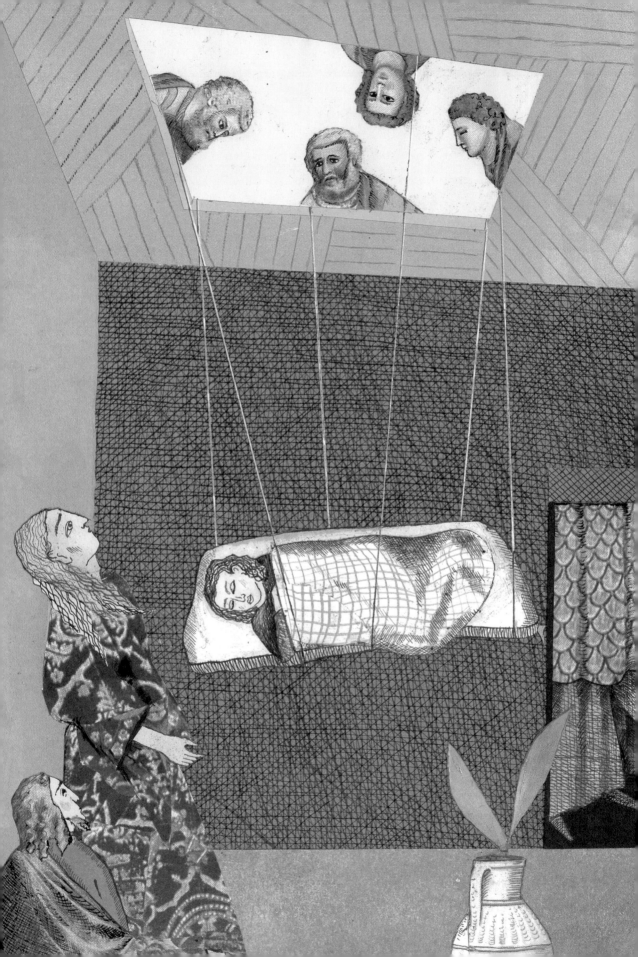

the room. The people in the house reached up to help bring the sick man safely to rest on the floor in front of Jesus.

Jesus saw the man lying before him perfectly still, not lifting his head or his hand. Then he looked up and saw the hopeful faces of the four friends looking down through the opening in the roof. He turned away from the crowd of people and spoke only to the ill man.

"Son, your sins are forgiven," he said.

There were some learned men sitting nearby who had come to hear what Jesus was teaching, and they asked themselves, "How can he say that? Only God can forgive sins." They didn't speak aloud but Jesus knew what they were thinking.

"Why do you question what I say?" he asked them. "God has given me the authority on earth to forgive sins. I will show you the power that I have." And he said to the ill man, "Stand up. Take up your bed and walk."

Immediately the man stood. He seemed not to see the people crowded around or the men looking down from the roof. He only heard Jesus' words, and he rolled up his sleeping mat and went home.

His friends came down from the roof and also left, rejoicing. Everyone who was there thanked God for what Jesus had done and the wonder they had seen.

CALMING THE STORM

Matthew 8.23-27;
Mark 4.35-41;
Luke 8.22-25.

ONE DAY Jesus had been preaching to a large crowd by the Sea of Galilee. When evening came he said to the disciples, "Let us go across to the other side."

So they got into a boat and prepared to sail. Jesus was tired from many hours of teaching so he lay down to rest on a pile of cushions in the stern of the boat. Soon he was asleep. The others raised the sails and the boat began to cross the water.

Suddenly the wind began to blow fiercely. It roared through the clefts in the hills around the sea, stirring up the water. In only a few minutes great waves were smashing over the boat, and it began to tilt and take on water. One of the disciples looked to be sure that Jesus was safe. He was sound asleep in the stern of the boat.

They shook him and woke him up.

"Teacher," they said. "How can you sleep in this storm? Don't you care that we are about to drown?"

Jesus stood up and looked at the raging sea. Then he spoke directly into the wind. "Peace!" he said. "Be still."

Immediately the wind stopped blowing and the water became calm. The boat righted itself and all was quiet.

Jesus turned to the disciples.

"Why are you afraid?" he asked. "Have you still no faith in what I can do?"

They were filled with great awe and said to one another, "It is true. Even the waves and the wind obey him." But still they could not truly understand what sort of man Jesus was.

JAIRUS' DAUGHTER

Matthew 9.18-26;
Mark 5.21-43;
Luke 8.40-56.

JESUS CAME BACK TO CAPERNAUM after a journey to the other side of the Sea of Galilee and found many people waiting to welcome him. Jairus, a leader of the synagogue, pushed his way through the throng and fell at his feet.

"Come to my house, Teacher," he said. "My only daughter is dying. She is a child, just twelve years old. I know that you can heal her."

Jesus went with Jairus toward his house and the crowd followed, pressing upon him. One woman managed to get close behind him. She had been sick with bleeding for twelve years, and though she had spent all her money on doctors, none had been able to cure her. She reached out and touched the edge of Jesus' robe. Immediately the bleeding stopped.

Jesus turned to Peter and said, "Who touched me?"

"Master," said Peter, "there are people all around you. Anyone might have touched you."

"Someone touched me because they needed help," said Jesus. "I felt the power go out from me."

The woman saw that she couldn't hide, and she came and knelt before him, trembling. She said, "I touched your robe and I was healed of bleeding that has afflicted me for twelve years."

Jesus said, "Your faith has made you well. Go in peace."

While he was still speaking, someone came through the crowd and said, "Jairus, your daughter is dead. Do not trouble the teacher any longer. There is nothing he can do."

Jairus was stricken with grief, but Jesus said, "Do not be afraid. Only believe and she will live."

When they came to the house it was surrounded by people weeping and musicians playing sad tunes. Jesus said to Peter, John and James, "Come with me," and they entered the house with Jairus and his wife.

Everyone in the house was wailing for the girl. Jesus said, "There is no need to mourn. She is not dead but sleeping." Some people laughed at him because they could see that Jairus' daughter was dead.

Jesus went to her. He took her hand and said, "Child, get up!" At once her spirit returned and she rose from her bed.

"Get this child something to eat," said Jesus.

Her parents were filled with joy and awe. They wanted to go out immediately and tell everyone what Jesus had done, but he said to them, "Do not speak of what has happened here. Stay at home and rejoice with your daughter."

JESUS INSTRUCTS THE DISCIPLES

JESUS WENT TO VILLAGES and towns across Galilee, teaching and curing every sickness. The crowds were so large that it was hard to help all who came, but he felt compassion for the people. They had many troubles and no one to turn to for help.

Matthew 9.35-38, 10.1-41, 11.1; Luke 10.3-12.

As he rested with his followers at the end of a day, he said to them, "These people are like sheep without a shepherd. We must ask God for more workers to go among them to teach them and help them."

And so he called together the twelve he had chosen as his disciples: Simon Peter and his brother Andrew; James and John, the sons of Zebedee; Philip and Bartholomew; Thomas and Matthew the tax collector; Thaddaeus and James the son of Alphaeus; Simon the Canaanite; and Judas Iscariot.

"You have heard my teaching and you have seen what I do in God's name. Now I am sending you out among the people to declare the good news of God's kingdom and to cure every sickness. You can do these things, for you will be able to act with my power," Jesus said to them.

"You will be doing the work of God and you must always keep this in mind. Take nothing with you, not even an extra pair of sandals. You will receive what you need. Remember

that you have not paid anything to receive the blessings of God, and you must not take payment for anything you do.

"When you arrive in a town, seek out a household of good and kind people and stay with them until it is time for you to continue on your journey. By the way you act and the words you say, bring peace upon the houses where you are welcomed.

"If a household or a town will not welcome you or will not listen to your words, leave and shake the dust of that place from your feet.

"Remember that there are some who will tell lies about you and try to hurt you because of the message you bring. Beware of them. Be as wise as serpents and as innocent as doves. If they question you, do not worry about what you should say. God will give you words to speak. And do not be afraid, for God notices when one sparrow falls, and you are of more value than many sparrows. God will always be with you.

"Remember that whoever welcomes you welcomes me and whoever welcomes me welcomes the one who sent me."

When Jesus had finished speaking he was ready to go on to more towns and villages to teach and heal, and the disciples knew that soon they, too, would be going out to do this work.

THE MAN WHO HELPED
A TRAVELER

Luke 10.29-37.

ONE DAY a lawyer was listening to Jesus teach. He said to him, "I have a question to ask you. You have said that I must love my neighbor as I love myself, but who is my neighbor? Is it someone who lives near me or someone who is like me in some way?"

To answer the question Jesus told this story.

A man from Jerusalem needed to travel to Jericho. He knew that the journey would be dangerous. The road was steep and treacherous and there were many robbers who lay in wait along the way. But he had to go and so he set out, hoping that he would arrive safely.

But, just as he had feared, he was attacked by men who took everything, even his clothes. They beat him and left him lying half dead by the road.

As the man lay there unable to move, a high priest from the temple in Jerusalem passed by. He was a very important person traveling on important business. He saw the injured man but he did not go over to help him. Instead he moved to the other side of the road and hurried past.

The next to come by was a Levite, one of the clerks of the temple – not as important as the priest but still a very busy man. He, too, turned his head away and passed by on the other side of the road.

Then a Samaritan came riding along on his donkey. Most of the Samaritan people lived in their own region to the north of Jerusalem, and they were not well looked on by the Jews, for they had their own temples and customs. But this Samaritan stopped his donkey when he saw the injured traveler. He got off and went to see if he could help.

When he saw that the man was unconscious and injured, the Samaritan took a bottle of wine and a bottle of oil from his bundles. He used the wine to wash the wounds and the oil to soothe them and he bound them up with strips of cloth.

Then he wrapped the man in his cloak, lifted him onto the back of his donkey and took him to the nearest inn. There he rented a room and tended the stranger until he was resting quietly.

The next day the Samaritan spoke to the innkeeper.

"I must leave to attend to some business," he said. "I ask you to look after this injured man until I can return. Here is money for your trouble. If you need to spend more to care for him, I will repay you."

He gave the innkeeper two denarii – as much as either of them could expect to earn in two days.

"I will do as you ask," said the innkeeper. He was a man who dealt with people of all kinds every day, and he believed that the Samaritan would keep his promise for he had cared for a stranger just as he would care for someone from his own village.

"Now," Jesus said to the lawyer, "which of the three passersby was a neighbor to the man who was robbed?"

"The one who helped him," answered the lawyer.

"Yes," said Jesus. "Go and do the same."

THE LOST SHEEP AND
THE LOST COIN

Luke 15.1-10;
Matthew 18.12-14.

A S JESUS TRAVELED the roads and paths of Galilee, all kinds of people came to hear what he had to say. Some tried their best to live righteously. Others had great trouble following the path they had been taught, and still others never seemed to try. Jesus welcomed them all.

Some people watched these crowds and sneered. They had no doubts that they themselves lived as they should because they knew the written law and always followed it most carefully. They said, "What kind of man is this who spends all his time with sinners and even eats with them?"

Jesus knew about these grumblings. One day he looked at all the people gathered near him, at the grumblers standing farther away, and beyond them to the hills, where they all lived in little villages and tended their flocks and their fields. He began to tell them stories.

"Imagine that you have a hundred sheep. One day you go out to the hills where the flock is grazing. You know your sheep well and immediately you see that one of them is gone. Don't you leave the ninety-nine to go and search everywhere for the one that is lost? And when you find it, don't you tell all your neighbors that your lost sheep, the one you were so worried about, has been found? In the same way I will search for one

[70]

lost soul and give thanks when that person begins to live as he should.

"Or think of a woman who has just ten precious silver coins. Perhaps they are the only coins that have ever been her own. If she loses one of these coins she will surely light a lamp so that her dark house is filled with light. Then she will sweep every corner until she finds what has been lost. And when she has the coin in her hand she will call together all her friends and say, 'Come and celebrate with me, for I have found the coin that I lost.' In the same way there is joy in heaven when one sinner repents.

"Such stories happen every day," said Jesus. "Look into your hearts and know that if you join the company of those who live as God wants them to live, you will be welcomed gladly."

THE LOST SON

ONE DAY Jesus told this story.

ONE DAY Jesus told this story. Luke 15.11-32.

There was a farmer who had two sons. He planned that his sons would share his fields and vineyards equally when he died.

But the younger son was restless and impatient.

"Father," he said, "give me my inheritance now, while I am young. I have plans of my own, things I want to do."

His father gave him his wish. He divided the property between the two sons. Within a few days the younger son had sold his part of the farm and gone off to a distant country with his pouch full of money.

Perhaps he meant to set himself up in business, but he fell in with people who cared nothing about work. He spent his money carousing with them all night and he slept all day. Soon all his money was gone and so were his friends. To make matters worse, there was a famine in the land and no one needed a young man who had forgotten how to work.

He left the city and went from one farm to the next saying, "I grew up working on my father's farm. Do you have something I could do?" But he no longer looked like a man who could do farm work, and it was a long time before he was hired

[*73*]

to feed pigs. He had very little to eat himself and he began to envy the pigs who were well fed.

"If only I could go back to my father," he thought. "A servant on his farm is far better off than I am now."

At last he decided that he must go home. As he traveled, becoming dustier and more ragged as he went, he thought about what he would say to his father.

"I'll tell him that I have sinned against heaven and against him. I will say, 'I am no longer worthy to be your son. Treat me as a hired hand. It is more than I deserve.'"

A servant saw him when he was far down the road and went to the farmer.

"Look," he said. "A stranger in ragged clothes is coming. Shall I send him away?"

But the old man knew his son at once and rushed to meet him. "Welcome, my son," he said and put his arms around him.

"Father, I am not worthy to be called your son," said the young man.

But the father would not listen. He said to the servant, "Bring my best robe and a ring for my son's finger and sandals for his feet. For this is not a stranger but my son who was lost and is found. Let us celebrate."

The older son was working in the field and no one told him that his brother had returned. When he came in from his day's work he was surprised to hear music and the sound of dancing and merry-making inside the house.

He called to one of the servants, "What is going on? What has happened?"

"The household is celebrating because your brother has come home," answered the servant.

The young man was angry when he heard this news. "Why should I join this celebration?" he said to himself, and he stood outside the door.

His father saw him and came to him.

"Come in," he said. "Your brother is here. Come and greet him."

The older son shook his head stubbornly.

"I have worked hard always," he said slowly. "I have done your bidding but you have never held a feast for me. I'm sure that my brother has come home with nothing. No doubt he wasted his money on high living. And yet you celebrate."

"You are with me always," said his father. "Every day I am glad of that. But today the son I thought I would never see again has returned. We must rejoice, for he was lost and now he is found. He was wrong but he is sorry, and we must welcome him."

Jesus looked at all the people around him. "So it is in the kingdom of heaven," he said. "The one who is lost is welcomed when he returns. You can be sure of that."

KNOCK AND THE DOOR
WILL BE OPENED

Luke 11.1-13.

JESUS TOLD THE DISCIPLES that it was important to pray, to ask God for their daily needs, for forgiveness and for protection. And he told them a story so that they would understand.

Suppose one night you have an unexpected guest. He has traveled a long way and he is hungry but it happens that you have no food in the house. You know that your friend next door has bread because his wife has done her baking that very day. It is late in the evening but surely your friend will not refuse you.

You go to his house. Already the door is locked and you know that inside the house the lamp has been put out and the family is lying on their sleeping platform with their sheep and goats asleep on the floor around them. But you must give your guest some food so you knock.

From inside your friend answers, "Don't bother me now. My children are asleep beside me and the house is dark. You can see that the door is locked. Go away and come back in the morning."

But you keep knocking because you know that he will understand when he hears that you must have bread to feed an unexpected guest. And finally he climbs over his sleeping fam-

ily and, in the dark, makes his way among the animals and unlocks the door. He gives you the bread you need.

So remember, ask and what you need will be given to you, search and you will find, knock and the door will be opened.

THE DEATH OF
JOHN THE BAPTIST

Matthew 14.3-13;
Mark 6.17-29.

As JESUS WENT ABOUT GALILEE teaching and healing, John the Baptist also continued his work baptizing and speaking against the sinful. Herod Antipas, the son of Herod the Great, now ruled Galilee. He had heard John preach and felt that he was a prophet.

But John angered Herod. He told the ruler that he had broken ancient law when he married his wife, Herodias.

"She was once the wife of your brother," John said. "Your brother still lives. You know that such a marriage is not lawful."

If Herod was angry, his wife was angrier. She wanted to kill John. But Herod feared John, for he knew that he was a righteous and holy man. So he put him in prison where Herodias could not reach him.

But Herodias waited for her chance.

It came when Herod gave a great banquet to celebrate his birthday. All of the courtiers and officers and leaders of Galilee were to attend. There would be fine food, wine and music.

Herodias said to her husband, "Let my daughter, Salome, entertain your guests. You know how beautifully she dances." And Herod agreed.

Salome was just a young girl and she was pleased to be

asked to dance at a grand feast. She prepared herself carefully. And the guests and Herod were pleased with her performance. They praised her greatly and Herod, feeling proud of the entertainment offered to the company, called Salome to him.

"Ask me for anything you wish and I will give it to you," he said.

"Anything?" said Salome.

"I swear before you and all my honored guests that I will give you whatever you want, even half of my kingdom."

"I am overcome," said Salome. "Let me go and think for a moment."

She went to her mother who was in a nearby room with other women.

"The guests praised my dancing," she said. "And Herod will give me anything I want. What should I ask for?"

Herodias drew a deep breath and said, "Tell him you want the head of John the Baptist."

Salome rushed back into the banquet hall and stood before Herod.

"I want you to give me the head of John the Baptist on a platter," she demanded.

Herod was appalled. He knew that John did not deserve to die but he had given an oath before his guests and he could not refuse. He called over one of the guards standing by the door.

"Go to the cell where John who baptizes is held and bring back his head," he ordered.

The soldier took his sword and obeyed the order. He returned with John's head on a platter and presented it to Salome. She took it to her mother.

News of the death of John traveled fast, and some of his followers came and took his body away and buried it in a tomb. Then they found Jesus and told him what had happened. Jesus immediately went by boat to a deserted place to pray and remember John.

LOAVES AND FISHES

Matthew 14.13-21;
Mark 6.32-44;
Luke 9.10-17;
John 6.1-14.

ONE DAY Jesus and the disciples took a boat and went to the eastern side of the Sea of Galilee. More than five thousand people came from nearby towns hoping to hear him and be healed.

When he saw the throng coming near, Jesus said to Philip, one of the disciples, "These people have brought nothing to eat. Where can we buy bread for all of them?" He already knew what he was going to do, but he wanted to hear what Philip would say.

"Master," said Philip, "there are thousands of people here. Six months' wages would not buy enough bread for each of them to have even a mouthful."

Andrew, the brother of Peter, said, "Here is a boy who has five barley loaves and two fishes he is willing to share. But that is nothing among so many."

"Tell the people to sit down on the grass," said Jesus. "And ask the boy to give me the food he has brought."

He took the loaves and the fishes in his hands and gave thanks. Then he began to break them into pieces for the disciples to distribute among the people. As long as there were men and women and children to be fed, the bread and fishes did not run out. There was plenty for everyone. When they had all

eaten as much as they wanted, Jesus told the disciples to gather up the scraps that were left so that nothing would be lost. The fragments filled twelve baskets.

When the people saw what Jesus had done they said to each other, "This man is indeed a prophet."

WALKING ON WATER

Matthew 14.22-36; Mark 6.45-52; John 6.16-21.

After Jesus had fed the five thousand people with bread and fish, he said to the disciples, "Get in the boat and go ahead to the other side of the lake. I will send the people on their way. Then I'll go up on the mountain to pray."

By the time he came back to the shore it was late at night. The disciples were still out on the lake, for a strong wind was preventing their boat from reaching the opposite shore. All night long they struggled.

When dawn broke they looked out over the choppy sea and saw a man walking toward them over the water.

They were terrified. No living person could walk on water.

"A ghost!" they cried. "It must be a ghost."

"No," said Jesus. "It is me. Do not be afraid."

The disciples knew his voice but still they were not sure.

Peter said, "Lord, if it is truly you, command me to walk to you over the water."

"Come," said Jesus.

Peter swung his legs over the side of the boat. He stood up and began to move toward Jesus. His feet stepped on the water just as they would on the land. Then he noticed how the wind was making the water rise and fall. Peter was frightened. How could the water hold him up? He began to sink.

"Lord, save me," he cried. Jesus immediately reached out and clasped his hand and held on to him strongly.

"You should have more faith, Peter," he said. "If you doubt me you will sink." And they walked together to the boat.

When they had climbed into the boat, the wind suddenly stopped blowing and the disciples said to Jesus, "Truly, you are the Son of God."

THE TRANSFIGURATION

Matthew 16.13-17.9;

Mark 8.27-9.10;

Luke 9.18-36.

JESUS AND HIS DISCIPLES were visiting villages around Caesarea Philippi. As they walked from one village to the next, he asked them, "What do you hear people saying about me? Who do they say I am?"

"Some say you are John the Baptist and others believe you are Elijah come again or one of the other prophets."

"But who do you say I am?"

Peter answered, "You are the Son of God."

Jesus looked at them all. Then he said, "I must tell you that a time is coming when I will be rejected and persecuted. I will undergo great suffering and in the end I will be killed, but after three days I will be alive again. I tell you this because I want you to know what will happen, but you must never speak of it to anyone else."

Peter drew him aside and said, "Don't tell us these things. They are too terrible to think about. They couldn't happen. They cannot be true."

Jesus turned away from him and said, "You are setting your mind on human things and refusing to believe what you don't want to believe. What I am telling you is the will of God."

Six days later Jesus took Peter, James and John with him up the slopes of a high mountain.

As they stood there together, the three disciples saw Jesus change. His face seemed to shine with light and his clothing became a dazzling white never seen on earth. And then they saw Moses and Elijah standing beside Jesus, talking with him.

Peter, James and John were awed and terrified. Peter spoke in a trembling voice, "Teacher, it is good that we are here with you. Let us make three shelters – one for you, one for Moses and one for Elijah."

Then a shimmering cloud came over them and a great voice from the cloud said, "This is my Son, the Beloved. Listen to him."

The disciples were overcome with fear and fell to the ground. Jesus bent over them and touched them.

"Get up," he said. "Do not be afraid." When they were standing again the cloud was gone and no one was there but Jesus, looking just as he had when they climbed the mountain.

As they walked down together, Jesus cautioned them again, "Tell no one what you have seen until after I have risen from the dead."

Peter, James and John obeyed him. They did not speak to others about what had happened on the mountain. But among themselves they talked, wondering what Jesus meant when he said that he would rise from the dead.

MARY AND MARTHA
AND LAZARUS

John 11.1-44

ARY AND MARTHA were sisters who lived in Bethany, a little town near Jerusalem. They knew Jesus well, for he had come to their house many times on his travels. They had welcomed him to their table and listened to his teachings, and they loved him.

Their brother Lazarus, who also lived in Bethany, became sick, and the sickness grew worse and worse. At last, fearing that he would die, Mary and Martha sent word telling Jesus that his friend was near death.

When he received the message Jesus said, "This illness is meant to bring glory to God. It will not end in death."

Though he loved Lazarus and his sisters, he did not go to them at once. He waited for two days and then said to his disciples, "It is time for me to go to Bethany. Our friend Lazarus has fallen asleep. I am going to awaken him."

The disciples said, "If he's asleep he'll wake up. He'll be all right."

Then Jesus told them plainly, "Lazarus has died, but I am glad that I did not go when Mary and Martha sent for me. When you see what I will do, you may learn to believe in me."

When Jesus and the disciples arrived in Bethany, Martha came out to meet them.

"Lazarus has been dead for four days," she said sadly. "If only you had been here, Lord, my brother would not have died."

"Your brother will be alive again," said Jesus.

"I know," said Martha. "We will all live again on the last day."

"He will live through me," said Jesus, "and so will anyone who believes in me."

Martha went to get Mary, and she came with friends who had been comforting her. They were all weeping. Jesus was deeply moved and he, too, began to weep.

"Where have you put Lazarus?" he asked.

They took him to a cave tomb where the body of Lazarus had been laid. There was a great stone in front of the opening.

"Take away the stone," said Jesus.

"But, Lord," said Martha, "he has been dead four days. There will be a terrible smell."

"I have told you," said Jesus, "that if you believe, you will see the wonders that God can do."

So they took the stone away and Jesus raised his eyes to heaven and prayed. When he had finished he called in a loud voice, "Lazarus, come out!"

In a moment, Lazarus walked out of the cave. He had been prepared for the grave so his face was wrapped in a cloth and his hands and feet were bound in strips of cloth, too.

All of the mourners were struck dumb with wonder. Then they began to praise Jesus, but he only said, "Now unbind Lazarus. Let him go home."

ZACCHAEUS
THE TAX COLLECTOR

Luke 19.1-10

THE ROMAN RULERS OF PALESTINE collected heavy taxes from all the people. The men who collected the taxes were generally hated because Rome was hated. Besides that, many tax collectors grew rich on the money they were allowed to keep. And people knew that they often became even richer by cheating.

In Jericho there was a rich tax collector named Zacchaeus who had heard of Jesus and was curious about him. One day someone told him that Jesus would be passing through the city on his way to Jerusalem, and so Zacchaeus went out into the crowded streets hoping to see the man everyone was talking about.

But Zacchaeus was a short man, and he soon realized that he would not be able to see over all the people. He knew by the excited voices in the crowd that Jesus was already not far away, so he ran ahead and climbed a sycamore tree and sat on a branch where he had a good view of the road.

He could see Jesus coming close and was congratulating himself on having such a good view when Jesus stopped and looked straight up at him. Then, to the tax collector's astonishment, Jesus spoke.

"Zacchaeus," he said, "hurry down from that tree for I must stay in your house today."

Zacchaeus climbed down quickly, happy to welcome Jesus as his guest. But many people in the crowd began to grumble.

"That man is a sinner," they said. "Why is Jesus going to stay with him?"

Zacchaeus heard them. He stood before Jesus and said, "Lord, I will give half of my possessions to the poor and if I have cheated anyone I will pay back four times as much as I have taken."

Then Jesus said to him, "I came to give you and other sinners a chance to repent the wrong things you have done. I know that you understand what you must do. As you welcomed me to your house, I welcome you to my father's house, the kingdom of God."

JESUS HEALS A BLIND MAN

John 7.10-44, 9.1-41.

JESUS WENT TO JERUSALEM during the Feast of Tabernacles, the great harvest festival when the people gathered to celebrate and give thanks. For a while nobody knew he was in the city, and as he went through the streets he could hear people talking about him. Some said, "He is a good man." But others thought he was deceiving people so that they would follow him.

After a few days Jesus went to the temple and began to teach. The temple officials were amazed at his understanding of the ancient law that had come down from Moses.

They said, "How can a simple man from Galilee who has never studied with scholars know so much?"

Jesus said to them, "My teaching is not mine. It comes from God who sent me into the world. I did not come to break the ancient law but to bring it to you as God would have you hear it."

Many people who were listening believed Jesus, but the officials were angry because he challenged their authority. They wanted to stop him from teaching but, for the time being, they could not.

As the festival came to an end, Jesus was walking with his disciples on the Sabbath when he stopped near a beggar who

had been blind since birth. Jesus spat on the ground and mixed the dust into mud. Then he spread the mud on the man's eyes.

"Go to the pool of Siloam," he said, "and wash the mud from your eyes."

The man did this and when the mud was gone, he could see. His neighbors noticed him walking boldly about and said, "Isn't that the blind man who used to sit and beg?"

Some said it was, but others said, "No, it is just someone who looks like him."

Then the man himself said, "Yes. I am the man who was blind. Now I can see!"

"How could this happen?" they asked. "Who has cured you?"

"A man called Jesus did it," he answered. "But I do not know where he is now."

They took the man to the temple officials, who made him tell the story again. After he had spoken they frowned and said, "Now we know that Jesus cannot be from God. It is against the ancient law to do any work on the Sabbath, and making mud is work."

But other people said, "He has done a wonderful thing. He must be a good man, for what he has done is good."

Again and again the officials questioned the man who had gained his sight. They even called in his parents and asked them whether their son had indeed been born blind.

Finally the man said, "You know nothing about Jesus but I do. I know that he healed me. I can see. He must be someone God listens to. He must be one who comes from God."

The officials were so angry and unwilling to believe him

that they threw him out of the temple. But Jesus heard what had happened. He found the man and spoke with him.

"I have come from God to bring his word to the people of the world," he said. "Do you believe that?"

"I believe," said the man.

THE GOOD SHEPHERD

John 10.11-18.

EVEN IN JERUSALEM many who came to hear Jesus were country people who spent their days tending their vineyards and their flocks of sheep and goats. He taught them with stories about the things they knew. One day when he was teaching in the city, he told them about the good shepherd.

"A good shepherd lays down his life for his sheep," Jesus said. "If a wolf comes, the shepherd confronts it and drives it away with his staff without thinking of the danger. A hired hand who is paid to look after the sheep will run away to save his own skin when he sees the wolf coming. He doesn't care about the sheep. When he is gone the wolf will come in and scatter the sheep and seize some of them and drag them away.

"I am the good shepherd. I care for my sheep. They follow me because they know my voice. I know them and they know me. There are other sheep who do not belong in my fold but they can come with me, too, and I will watch over them all.

"I will lay down my life for my sheep. I give my life of my own accord and I have the power to live again. This is what my Father has told me."

ENTRY INTO JERUSALEM

Matthew 21.1-11;
Mark 11.1-10;
Luke 19.29-40;
John 12.12-19.

AS NEWS OF THE MIRACLES and teachings of Jesus became well known in Jerusalem, some people rejoiced. But others were disturbed. They knew that Jesus often spoke against the need to follow the ancient laws exactly as they had been written, and they were afraid that he would undermine the traditional authority of the temple leaders. They also knew that he was sometimes surrounded by great crowds, and they worried that his followers might rise up in rebellion.

They said to each other, "If our Roman rulers hear that there is unrest among the people, they will fear an uprising against them. Then the Roman soldiers will come and destroy us all."

Some of these people began to think that Jesus was a threat and must die.

Jesus knew that danger awaited him in Jerusalem, but he was determined to go. It was only in the holy city that the authorities could accept him as a true teacher of God's word. He also knew that it was prophesied that he would suffer and die in Jerusalem and that he must go.

Passover, the festival celebrating the escape of the Israelites from slavery in Egypt, was approaching, and the city would be crowded with people who might be ready to hear him. So he

[*106*]

set out from Galilee with the disciples and a group of other men and women.

As they came near the city, Jesus stopped beside the Mount of Olives. He called two of his disciples and said to them, "Go into the village just ahead and you will see a donkey with a colt. Untie the colt and bring it to me. If anyone asks why you are taking the colt, just say this, 'The Lord needs it and will send it back very soon.'"

And indeed they found a colt tied near a door. As they were untying it some people saw them and asked them what they were doing. The disciples told them what Jesus had said, and they were allowed to take the colt away. They brought it to Jesus and put their cloaks over its back. Jesus sat on the donkey and rode into Jerusalem.

As he came along the road down from the Mount of Olives, his followers and others along the way began to shout joyfully, "Hosanna! Blessed is the one who comes in the name of the Lord! Hosanna to the highest heaven!"

Some people in the crowd called out, "Teacher, order your disciples to stop shouting!"

Jesus answered, "If these voices were silent, the stones themselves would shout out. You cannot silence this news."

Word of what was happening spread quickly and the crowd grew. Some people asked, "Who is this man?" Others told them, "This is the prophet Jesus from Nazareth in Galilee."

As Jesus rode through the streets of Jerusalem, many people came and spread their cloaks or laid leafy branches on the ground before him, and the shouts of hosanna echoed from the walls and rose to the heavens.

JESUS IN THE TEMPLE

Matthew 21.12-13,
21.23-27, 22.15-22,
22.34-40;
Mark 11.15 11.19,
11.27-33, 12.13-19,
12.28-34;
Luke 19.45-48,
20.1-8, 20.22-26;
John 2.13-16.

THE TEMPLE IN JERUSALEM was a magnificent building surrounded by courtyards. The outer courtyards were always crowded with people who had come to pray, to make petitions and to make sacrifices of money, wheat, fruit or animals. Because people came to the temple from all around the Mediterranean, money changers set up tables so that travelers could change the money they brought into the coinage that was accepted by the temple. There were also vendors selling birds to be sacrificed.

Jesus believed that buying and selling should be done somewhere else, not in the holiest of places, so when he was in Jerusalem for Passover he went to the temple. He said to the people there, "In the scriptures it says, 'My house shall be called a house of prayer for people of all races.' Yet you have turned it into a robbers' cave."

Then he turned over the tables of the money changers and the chairs of those who were selling doves. And he would not let anyone bring anything to sell into the courtyards.

When the temple authorities heard of this and saw that the crowd was spellbound by what Jesus said, they became even more determined to kill him.

That evening Jesus and his followers went out of the city to sleep, but in the morning he returned to the temple to teach.

The chief priests and others came to him and said, "Who gave you the authority to speak as you do and interfere with the business of the temple?"

Jesus said, "I will ask you one question. Answer it and I will tell you by what authority I do these things. Did the power of John to baptize come from heaven or was it of human origin? Answer me."

His questioners stood in a little group and argued with one another.

"If we say from heaven, he will say, 'Then why did you not believe him?' If we say of human origin, then the crowd will be angry, for they believe John was a prophet."

In the end they turned to Jesus and said, "We do not know."

"Since you have not answered my question," said Jesus, "I will not tell you by what authority I do what I do."

Some other learned men came and said to him, "Teacher, we know you are sincere and teach what you believe without favoring anyone. So tell us, is it right to pay taxes to Rome or should we refuse to pay because we owe nothing except to God."

Jesus knew they were trying to trap him into saying something that would anger the Roman authorities, so he said, "Bring me a denarius, a coin of this country." They brought him one and he held it up and asked, "Whose head is on this coin?"

"The emperor's, of course," they answered.

"The coin comes from the emperor," said Jesus. "It has

nothing to do with God. Give the emperor the things that are the emperor's, and God the things that are God's."

A temple scribe asked him another question to test him. "Which commandment is the most important of all?"

Jesus answered, "'You shall love the Lord your God with all your heart and soul and mind and strength.' That is the first and greatest commandment. And the second is, 'Love your neighbor as yourself.' There are no other commandments greater than these."

The man said, "Teacher, you are right. It is most important to love God and to love your neighbor. These things are much more important than burnt offerings and sacrifices."

Jesus said, "You are not far from the kingdom of God."

After that no one dared to try to catch him with questions.

THE LAST SUPPER

Matthew 26.17-29;
Mark 14.12-25;
Luke 22.7-30.

WHEN THE DAY for the Passover feast came, Jesus sent Peter and John into the city.

"Go and prepare the meal of bitter herbs and roast lamb and unleavened bread so we can all eat it together," he said.

"But where shall we make these preparations?" they asked. They wanted to make sure that the place for the feast was safe. The authorities were becoming more and more fearful of Jesus' power with the people. They might come to arrest him at any time.

"I will tell you what to do," Jesus said. "When you enter the city you will meet a man carrying a jar of water."

The disciples nodded. It was unusual for a man to carry water, so the jar of water would be a sign.

"Follow him," Jesus went on. "Enter the house he enters and say to the owner of the house, 'The teacher asks for a room where he may eat the Passover with his disciples.' He will show you a large room upstairs. Prepare the meal for us there."

When evening came, Jesus and the rest of the disciples arrived to find the feast ready. They sat on rugs around the low table and prepared to eat.

Jesus said to them, "I have been looking forward to having this meal with you before things happen that will take me away from you for a time. We will not eat and drink together like this until we meet in my Father's kingdom."

And so while they ate the Passover food and drank the wine, they spoke of many things that had happened in their travels together, and the disciples listened to Jesus' voice and the words he said.

When there was nothing left but bread and wine, Jesus took bread and broke it into pieces. He gave a piece to each disciple, saying, "This is my body which I will give for you. I ask you to gather together when I am gone and remember me by doing as we do now." And they each ate the bread.

Then Jesus poured wine into the cup of each disciple and said, "This is my blood given to pledge new faith between you and God. I ask you to gather together when I am gone and remember me by doing as we do now." And they drank the wine.

Then Jesus looked around the table and said, "Tonight one of you will betray me and deliver me to the authorities."

The disciples were terribly distressed. They looked at each other and wondered which one of them could do this terrible thing.

Jesus said, "Woe to the one who will betray the Son of God. But the rest of you have stood by me in all my trials, and you will eat and drink with me when you come to be with me in my kingdom."

IN THE GARDEN OF
GETHSEMANE

Matthew 26.30-56;
Mark 14.32-50;
Luke 22.39-53. WHEN THE PASSOVER FEAST WAS OVER, Jesus and the disciples went to Gethsemane, a garden on the Mount of Olives, and found a quiet place away from other people.

"I will take Peter and James and John with me while I pray," said Jesus.

The others sat down on the ground to wait. But one of them, Judas Iscariot, slipped away in the darkness and went to tell the authorities where to find Jesus, for they had promised him thirty silver coins for betraying his master.

Peter, James and John could see that Jesus was deeply troubled. He said to them, "I am sad to the depth of my soul. Please sit here near me and stay awake until I come back." Then he went a little way off and threw himself on the ground and prayed, "Father, for you all things are possible. I would ask you to take away this hour when I must die. But what I want does not matter. It is what you want that must be done."

When he had prayed, he came back to the three disciples and found them all asleep.

"Peter!" he said. "Couldn't you stay awake with me even one hour? You should be praying that you will not have to go through terrible trials. Your spirit is willing but your body is weak."

[*118*]

Again he went away and prayed, "My Father, if this must happen to me, your will be done."

The three tried to stay awake but their eyes were very heavy and they fell asleep once more. When Jesus returned, they did not know what to say to him.

A third time he went to pray. This time when he came back he said, "Sleeping again? It is enough. The time has come when I will be given to my enemies. Get up, it is time to go. See, my betrayer is at hand."

The disciples opened their eyes to see a mob of people with swords and clubs coming toward them, and with them was one of their own company, Judas Iscariot. He came directly to Jesus and said, "Teacher!" and gave him the kiss of friendship, for this was the signal he had arranged with Jesus' enemies.

So Jesus was arrested. But one of his supporters drew his sword and struck a guard and cut off his ear.

Jesus said, "Put away your sword, for if you use the sword you will die by the sword. Don't you know that I can ask my Father for help? He would send twelve legions of angels, but this is what I must do now." Then he said to the guards, "Day after day I sat teaching in the temple and you did not arrest me. Now you come in the night with swords and clubs as if I were a bandit. But I will go with you because this has been prophesied and must take place."

When the disciples saw that Jesus was being bound and taken away, they were afraid, and they ran into the city to hide.

PETER

ALL OF THE DISCIPLES except Judas Iscariot wanted to be faithful to Jesus, and they promised him that they would never desert him. But Jesus knew that they were human. He understood that they would be frightened and confused when he was arrested and they would run away in spite of their promises.

Matthew 26.31-35, 26.57-58, 26.69-75; Mark 14.29-31, 14.66-72; Luke 22.31-34, 22.54-62; John 13.37-38, 18.15-18, 18.25-27.

Among all of them Peter was the most sure that he would be faithful. He was always willing to step forward and pledge himself to his beloved teacher. Before Jesus went to pray in the garden of Gethsemane, Peter said to him, "Even if the others desert you, I will stand by you always."

But Jesus knew that Peter's courage often failed him even though his heart was true.

"Peter," he answered, "I tell you truly that before the cock crows this night, you will deny me three times."

"No!" said Peter. "I will not deny you, even if it means I must die with you."

Jesus looked at Peter with love, though he knew that his most trusted disciple would not be able to keep his promise. And indeed, when the guards came and took Jesus for trial, Peter ran away with the other disciples.

But he did not go with the others to a place of hiding. As

Jesus was taken to the house of the high priest, Peter followed the crowd. He joined the group of guards who were gathered around a fire in the courtyard and waited to see what would happen next.

After a while a young servant girl came up to him and said, "You were with Jesus the Galilean, weren't you?"

"No," said Peter. "Why would you say that? I don't know what you're talking about." But he turned away from the fire and moved to the edge of the courtyard.

Another servant girl looked at him carefully and said to the people who were waiting, "This man was with Jesus of Nazareth. I saw them together."

"Never! I swear it," said Peter. "I don't know the man."

After a little while one of the bystanders came up to him and said, "I've been listening to you and I know by your accent that you are one of the Galileans."

Peter began to curse. "I tell you again. I do not know this man."

Just then a cock crowed. When he heard that sound, Peter remembered what Jesus had said: "Before the cock crows this night, you will deny me three times."

Peter was silent. Then he left the courtyard and stood in the street and wept bitterly.

THE TRIAL AND CRUCIFIXION
OF JESUS

Matthew 27.1-56;
Mark 14.60-65,
15.1-41;
Luke 22.54-23.49;
John 18.19-23.

THE HIGH PRIEST and other temple officials questioned Jesus for many hours, trying to find a reason to have him killed.

Jesus said to them, "I have always spoken openly in the world. I have taught in the synagogues and in the temple and I have said nothing in secret. If you want to know what I have said, ask those who have heard me."

One of the guards struck him in the face, saying, "Is this how you answer the high priest?"

Jesus said, "Unless you have evidence that what I say is false, why do you strike me?"

They called for witnesses to testify against Jesus, to say that he had spoken against the established authority. Some came and testified falsely, but their lies did not agree with each other and so they proved nothing.

Then the high priest said, "Are you the Son of God?"

"I am," said Jesus, "and you will see me seated at the right hand of God and coming with the clouds of heaven."

"It is blasphemy to claim to be the Son of God," said the high priest. "You have all heard it. It is time to make a decision about this man."

Everyone there agreed that Jesus deserved to die, and they began to spit on him and strike him.

"You say you are a prophet," they jeered. "If you are a prophet, then prophesy. We might let you go."

In the early morning they took him to Pilate, the Roman governor, for execution.

"I hear that you claim to be the king of the Jewish people of this realm," said Pilate.

"If you say so," said Jesus.

Pilate then listened to a long list of accusations brought by the temple authorities.

"What do you say in answer to all of these charges?" he asked.

Jesus said nothing. When Pilate questioned him again he still said nothing.

Pilate was amazed at his silence, for he could see that the temple authorities were afraid of the power of Jesus and his teaching.

"I can see no reason to execute this man," he said, "but I will leave it to the people."

It was his custom to free one criminal at the time of Passover and to let the people of Jerusalem choose the one to be freed. In the prison there was a well-known criminal called Barabbas. Even though he was a murderer, he was popular with the people because he often defied Roman authority.

Pilate asked the crowd, "Which one shall I free — Barabbas, or Jesus called the Son of God?"

The temple officials had made sure that the crowd was whipped up against Jesus. "Free Barabbas!" they cried out.

"Then what do you want me to do with Jesus?"

"Crucify him!" they answered.

"Why? What wrong has he done?" asked Pilate.

But the crowd only shouted louder, "Crucify him!"

When Pilate saw that the crowd would riot if he did not do as they demanded, he had a bowl of water brought to him. There, in front of them all, he washed his hands and said, "My hands are clean. I am not responsible for this man's death."

Then the Roman soldiers took Jesus and beat him. They put a cloak on him and piled branches of thorns on his head.

"Now you are a crowned king, as you claim to be," they said, and they mocked him and spat on him.

At about nine o'clock in the morning, the soldiers led Jesus out to a bleak field called Golgotha, which means the place of the skull, to be crucified. They nailed him by his hands and his feet to a cross made of wood. They set the cross up and waited for him to die. Two robbers were crucified with him, one on either side.

The soldiers who were guarding the place cast lots for Jesus' cloak and sandals and kept an eye on the passersby. Some people came to jeer.

"You saved others," they yelled. "Can't you save yourself? Where is God your Father now?"

But others were there, too, among them Jesus' mother, Mary, and some other women who had come from Galilee. Jesus saw his mother standing by one of the disciples and he said to her, "Look, here is one who will be a son to you now." And to the disciple he said, "Here is your mother." From then on the disciple took Mary into his own house to live.

At noon darkness came over the land, and at three o'clock Jesus cried out in a loud voice, "Father, into your hands I give my spirit." Then he died.

At that moment the curtain of the temple was torn in two from top to bottom. The earth shook and rocks split. The Roman soldier who stood facing Jesus and saw how he died said, "What this man said was true. He was the Son of God."

THE BURIAL AND
RESURRECTION OF JESUS

THERE WAS A GOOD AND JUST MAN called Joseph of Arimathea, who followed Jesus in secret because he feared the power of the temple officials. After Jesus died and was taken from the cross, Joseph went to Pilate and was given permission to take away the body and bury it.

Matthew 27.57-60, 28.1-10;
Mark 15.42-16.11;
Luke 23.50-24.12;
John 19.38-20.18.

As was the custom among those who could afford it, Joseph had a tomb ready for himself and his family in a cave in a garden not far from Golgotha. It had never been used. Nicodemus, another secret follower, brought a mixture of myrrh and aloes. Together the two men prepared the body of Jesus for burial by wrapping it with the spices in linen cloths. Then they laid the body in the prepared tomb and put a large rock before the cave opening.

On the third day after the burial, Mary of Magdala, a follower of Jesus, came to pray at the tomb very early in the morning. She saw at once that the stone at the opening of the cave had been moved aside. Alarmed, she peered in, but it was still too dark for her to see anything. She ran to Peter and another disciple and said, "I am afraid that someone has taken the Lord from the tomb and I don't know where they have laid him."

The two disciples ran to the tomb. It was lighter now and

[*129*]

from the opening they could see that the linen wrappings were there, still wound together, but Jesus was gone. When they went inside they found the cloth that had been around his head rolled up and lying apart from the other linen.

Then they knew that Jesus' body had not been taken away to another place. He had risen from the dead and gone away, leaving his burial cloths behind.

Peter and the other disciple returned to the place where they were staying, too overwhelmed to speak of what they did not truly understand. Mary saw them go as she stood weeping beside the tomb, still thinking that someone had taken the body away.

At last she bent to look inside, and she saw two angels in white who sat in the place where Jesus' body had lain, one at the head and the other at the foot.

"Woman, why are you weeping?" they said to her.

"Because someone has taken my Lord away and I don't know where to find him." Then she turned and saw Jesus standing near her, but she did not recognize him.

"Why are you crying," he asked. "Who are you looking for?"

Mary thought he was the gardener and she said to him, "Please, sir. If you have carried him away, tell me where he is."

Then Jesus said, "Mary!" and she recognized his voice.

"Teacher!" she said and reached out to touch him.

"I cannot stay with you now," said Jesus. "I have not yet gone up to my Father. Go and tell my disciples that I am returning to the one who is my Father and your Father, my God and your God." And then he was gone.

So Mary of Magdala went in great joy to the disciples and said, "I have seen our Lord, and he lives." Then she told them all that she had seen and all that Jesus had said.

ON THE ROAD TO EMMAUS

Luke 24.13-35.

ON THE SAME DAY that Mary of Magdala found the empty tomb, two of Jesus' followers were walking to Emmaus, a village about seven miles from Jerusalem. They walked slowly, talking together about the trial and death of their teacher. As they wondered what would happen now, Jesus himself came along the road and walked beside them. They saw him but they did not recognize him.

"What are you talking about so seriously?" he asked.

They stopped and looked at him sadly, but even then they did not see that it was Jesus standing before them.

Finally one of the men said, "You must be the only stranger in Jerusalem who has not heard of all the things that have happened in these past days."

"What has happened?" said Jesus.

They began to tell him about Jesus from Nazareth and his wondrous words and deeds and how he had died.

"We hoped he would rise from the dead and come to bring us a new life," they said. "But he has been dead for three days now. We have heard that someone saw a vision of angels who said he is alive. But when others went to the tomb it was empty."

Jesus shook his head and said, "Oh, how foolish you all are.

Don't you believe what the prophets have said?" And he began to explain to them how Moses and all the prophets had foretold that the Son of God would die and rise again.

As they drew near to Emmaus, Jesus began to walk ahead as if he meant to go on, but the two men stopped him. Somehow they did not want this stranger to leave them.

"It's almost evening and it will be dark soon," they said to him. "Come and stay with us."

So Jesus went with them into the house where they were going to stay. Soon they sat at a table together and food was put before them. The two men saw the stranger take up bread and bless it. Then he broke the bread and gave a piece to each of them.

Suddenly their eyes were opened and they recognized Jesus. But just as they were about to speak, he vanished from their sight.

The two men looked at each other. "When he spoke to us on the road my heart rejoiced," one said.

Yes," said the other. "And he made the teachings of the prophets clear. No other teacher can do that so well."

They rose from the table and went at once to Jerusalem, where they found the disciples and other followers of Jesus all together. They told the story of their walk to Emmaus and how Jesus had spoken to them and how he had made himself known to them in the breaking of bread.

THE RISEN JESUS

Luke 24.36-52;
John 20.19-29,
21.1-19.

ON THE THIRD DAY after the crucifixion, two men were talking with Jesus' disciples and their companions. With awe and excitement they were speaking of how they had just met Jesus on the road to Emmaus. Suddenly they stopped talking, for Jesus was standing in the room with them. All the others were startled and terrified.

Some of them said, "It must be a ghost." The others agreed. "What else could it be," they whispered.

Jesus said, "Why are you frightened? Why do you have doubts? Look at my hands and feet. Touch me. A ghost does not have flesh and bones. I do."

They touched him and saw that there were nail holes in his hands and feet.

While they were still staring in wonder, Jesus said, "Have you anything I could eat?" They gave him a piece of broiled fish and he ate it.

When he had eaten he said to them, "You are witnesses to all that has happened." And he reminded them of things he had told them in their time together and all the prophecy that had been fulfilled.

Then he led them out of Jerusalem as far as Bethany, where he lifted up his hands and blessed them. While he was still blessing them he drew away, and they saw him being carried into heaven.

All of the disciples and followers returned to Jerusalem with great joy, thanking God.

Now, Thomas had not been with the other disciples when Jesus came to them. They told him everything that had happened but Thomas said, "Unless I see the wounds of the nails in his hands and put my fingers into those wounds I will not believe."

A week later all of the disciples were together in the house where they were staying. The doors were shut and fastened but suddenly Jesus stood among them.

He said to all of them, "Peace be with you." Then he spoke to Thomas. "Look at my hands and put your fingers into the holes the nails made. Do not doubt but believe."

Thomas did as he asked and then he said, "My Lord and my God. Now I know it is you."

Jesus said, "Could you not believe without seeing me? Blessed are those who are able to believe though they have not seen."

After some time had passed, many of the disciples returned to their homes in Galilee. One day Peter went fishing near the town of Tiberias. Several of the others, including Thomas, James and John, said, "We will go with you."

They stayed out in the boat all night but they caught nothing.

Just after daybreak they came into shore and saw a man standing there.

He said to them, "Children, I see that you have caught no fish."

They said, "You're right. We have fished all night for nothing."

"Cast your net on the right side of the boat," he said. "You will get some fish."

They took the boat out into the lake again and did as he said. So many fish came into the net that they could not haul it into the boat.

One of the disciples looked at Peter and said, "It is the Lord."

They brought the boat in, dragging the net full of fish. When they came ashore they saw that Jesus had built a fire. There was fish on it and bread.

Jesus said, "We will need more fish. Bring some of those you have caught."

Peter hauled the net up onto the shore. There were one hundred and fifty-three large fish in it, yet the net was not torn.

Jesus said, "Come and have breakfast." He cooked the fish and gave them bread and fish to eat.

When they had finished eating, Jesus said to Peter, "Do you love me more than you love any others?"

Peter answered, "Yes, Lord. You know that I love you."

Jesus said to him, "Feed my lambs." Then he asked him a second time, "Simon Peter, son of John, do you love me?"

Again Peter answered, "Yes, Lord. You know that I love you."

Jesus said to him, "Tend my sheep." Then he asked him a third time, "Do you love me?"

Peter felt hurt that Jesus would question him in this way.

"Lord," he said, "you know everything. You surely know that I love you."

Jesus said to him, "I do know that you love me and so I ask you to care for my followers, my sheep, even though it brings you grief and trouble."

And Peter did care for the followers of Jesus. In the time to come he told many people about Jesus and they, too, became followers.

This was the third time that Jesus appeared to the disciples after he rose from the dead.